■K READERS

Level 3

Level 4

A Note to Parents

DK READERS is a compelling program for beginning readers, designed in conjunction with leading literacy experts, including Dr. Linda Gambrell, Professor of Education at Clemson University. Dr. Gambrell has served as President of the National Reading Conference, the College Reading Association, and the International Reading Association.

Beautiful illustrations and superb full-color photographs combine with engaging, easy-to-read stories to offer a fresh approach to each subject in the series. Each DK READER is guaranteed to capture a child's interest while developing his or her reading skills, general knowledge, and love of reading.

The five levels of DK READERS are aimed at different reading abilities, enabling you to choose the books that are exactly right for your child:

Pre-level 1: Learning to read
Level 1: Beginning to read
Level 2: Beginning to read alone
Level 3: Reading alone
Level 4: Proficient readers

The "normal" age at which a child begins to read can be anywhere from three to eight years old. Adult participation through the lower levels is very helpful for providing encouragement, discussing storylines, and sounding out unfamiliar words.

No matter which level you select, you can be sure that you are helping your child learn to read, then read to learn!

LONDON, NEW YORK, MUNICH,
MELBOURNE, AND DELHI

For DK Publishing
Editor Lisa Stock
Designer Owen Bennett
Managing Art Editor Ron Stobbart
Managing Editor Catherine Saunders
Art Director Lisa Lanzarini
Publishing Manager Simon Beecroft
Category Publisher Alex Allan
Production Editor Sean Daly
Production Controller Rita Sinha
Reading Consultant Dr. Linda Gambrell

For Lucasfilm
Executive Editor J. W. Rinzler
Editor Frank Parisi
Art Director Troy Alders
Keeper of the Indycron Leland Chee
Director of Publishing Carol Roeder

First published in the United States in 2011 by DK Publishing
375 Hudson Street, New York, New York 10014

11 12 13 14 15 10 9 8 7 6 5 4 3 2 1

DK books are available at special discounts when purchased in bulk
for sales promotions, premiums, fund-raising, or educational use.
For details, contact:
DK Publishing Special Markets
375 Hudson Street, New York, New York 10014
SpecialSales@dk.com

A catalog record for this book is available
from the Library of Congress.

ISBN 978-0-7566-7135-8 (Paperback)
ISBN 978-0-7566-7136-5 (Hardcover)

Color reproduction by Media Development and Printing Ltd, UK
Printed and bound in China by L.Rex

Discover more at
www.dk.com
www.indianajones.com

Contents

DK READERS

READING ALONE 3

INDIANA JONES

GREAT ESCAPES

Written by W. Rathbone

Dr. Jones

This is Indiana Jones. His real name is Dr. Henry Jones Junior, but he prefers to be called Indiana or Indy because he once had a beloved dog of that name. By either name, Indiana has had many exciting and dangerous adventures. During his career as an archaeologist, Indy has been to exotic places and often met horrible villains. Many times, he has barely escaped with his life.

In the classroom
Away from his adventures, Indy spends most of his time teaching. He makes the lectures come alive for his students because he often has first-hand knowledge of the subject he is discussing.

Life experience

The key to escape is often experience. During Indy's many years of adventures he has learned how to survive in the face of danger. It also helps that he has good instincts and a lot of luck.

Indy finds the golden idol.

Indy is exploring an ancient temple in Peru. He is looking for a golden idol. Experience tells him just grabbing the idol looks too easy. It must be a trap!

Sacred golden idol
The golden idol is a carving of the ancient Chachapoyan goddess of fertility. The Chachapoyan people lived in the cloud forests of Peru.

Of course, Indy is right and he has to run for his life. First he must dodge poison darts and then he has to outrun a massive boulder. A last-minute leap is the only thing that saves Indy from being crushed like a bug!

Constant danger

Escaping is rarely easy. Dr. Jones sometimes survives one adventure but then has to face another straight away! In Peru, Indy avoids the temple's traps and escapes with the idol. However, more dangers are waiting outside.

Indy's enemy, René Belloq, snatches
the golden idol from his hands and orders
his Hovitos warriors to kill Indy. Indy runs
away through a perilous jungle and an
open field. He finally makes it to where
his trusted friend Jock is waiting for him.
They both escape to
safety in Jock's biplane.

Hovitos warriors
The Hovitos are descendants
of the ancient Chachapoyans.
Belloq tricks them into thinking
that Indy is their enemy.

Self-defense

Young Indy fought in the trenches during World War I. This ordeal made him determined to learn how to defend himself against his enemies, so Indy became a weapons expert. Now he can skillfully fire anything he gets his hands on.

Indy faces a fierce assassin.

Facing an assassin who has a scimitar, Indiana knows exactly how to defend himself with his pistol.

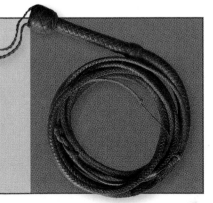

Reliable weapon
Indy sometimes has trouble finding ammunition for his pistol, but luckily he can always rely on his trusty bullwhip.

Indy can't use the bazooka because the Ark is in his line of fire.

On the trail of the Ark of the Covenant, Indy picks up another firearm—a bazooka. However, his Nazi enemies manage to sneak up behind him and take Indy prisoner.

Indy is also handy with a sword.

Whip at work

Indiana Jones often finds himself in unusual situations. For those moments he has an unusual tool to help him fight off enemies: a whip. While searching for the sacred Sankara Stones, Indy is attacked and has to wield his whip against an assassin to escape.

His trusty whip has other uses too. On the trail of the Holy Grail, Indy uses it to swing from one room and crash through the window of another. This is probably not the safest way to travel!

Indy's whip is a useful tool.

Useful friends

Loyal friends put themselves in the path of danger to help Indy escape.

Indy has found the ashes of a legendary emperor and some gangsters want to get their hands on them. His old friend Wu Han disguises himself as a waiter at Club Obi Wan.

He tries to guard Indy during a meeting with the gangsters.

Wu Han helps Indy, but pays with his life.

Marion Ravenwood
Marion is the great love of Indy's life. She is feisty and loves adventure almost as much as he does. One day Marion will marry Dr. Jones.

Having friends also means helping them out when they are in trouble. When brutal Nazi agent Arnold Toht takes Marion Ravenwood prisoner, Indiana Jones puts his own life at risk by returning to rescue his friend. In the fight that follows, Indy saves Marion and also recovers an invaluable headpiece.

Two thugs hold Marion prisoner.

Young Indy carries his friend out of a burning pirate ship.

Heavy burden

It can be hard enough for Indy to escape, but when he has a companion it is an even tougher task. Before he can break out of a snake-infested Egyptian tomb, Indy has to catch his friend Marion who is thrown down there by an evil Nazi.

Another battle with Toht and his thugs creates a huge fire that burns down the Raven tavern. Indy has to escape the burning building and save Marion. Standing in the smoke and debris, Marion tells Indy that she is now his new partner in adventure!

Taken by surprise

Danger and rescue can come in unlikely forms. While racing for the Ark of the Covenant, Indy is betrayed by a monkey. The sneaky monkey shows the Nazis where his friend Marion is hiding.

Mean Monkey
This cute Capuchin monkey befriends Marion but is actually working for the Nazis.

Children can also be unlikely rescuers. After the Nazis find Marion, Belloq and his henchmen try to attack Indy in a crowded café. Indy's friend Sallah sends in his children to help. The kids not only help Indy escape, but they also give him hope that he will find Marion again.

Ups and downs

Indy is often fighting with enemies who are hard to beat. These battles have their ups and downs. Indy may be losing, then winning—and then losing again. He may win easily or he may barely get away with his life. Often it is not even a fair fight, with Indy having to take on more than one bad guy at a time!

Indy is losing this fight, but the tank is about to roll off a cliff and only he will survive.

After Nazis kidnap his dad, Indy has to fight against tanks and truckloads of bad guys. One Nazi tries to whack Indy with a shovel. Fortunately, Indy is very good with his fists and is able to save his father.

Henry is relieved to see that his son has not plummeted to his doom.

Mola Ram

Indy's foes

Dr. Jones has come up against many villains: Walter Donovan wants the Holy Grail, Mola Ram hunts the Sankara

Walter Donovan

Stones. René Belloq dreams of finding the Ark and Irina Spalko uses Indy to find the Crystal Skull. However, none of them are able to beat Indy.

Irina Spalko

René Belloq

Bitter enemy

Indy faces one enemy again and again—the Nazis. During World War II, the Nazis control Germany.

Arnold Toht is a dangerous Nazi

They are on the hunt for mysterious legendary items, which they think will help them win the war. Indiana wants to stop them.

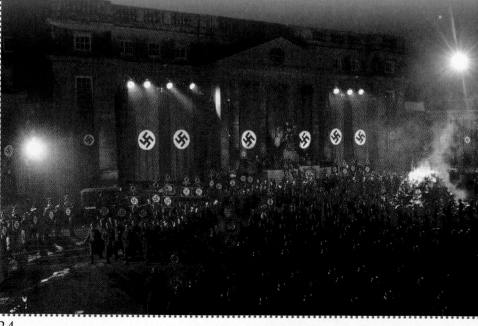

Nazis have possession of the Ark, but Indy will get it back!

Indy goes up against the Nazis during the search for the Ark of the Covenant. Later the Nazis want to find the sacred Holy Grail. Fortunately, Indy outsmarts them on both occasions.

Holy Grail

The Holy Grail is a cup believed to have been used by Jesus. It is supposed to have miraculous powers.

Dangerous potions

The enemies of Indiana Jones can be diabolical. He has to find ways to defeat their evil magic before it is too late.

In Transylvania, young Indy met a vampire known as Vlad the Impaler. He forced Indy to drink a poisonous potion, but Indy managed to get away and destroy the vampire.

Years later, Dr. Jones meets Thuggee leader Mola Ram. He gives Indy another awful potion to turn him into a zombie. Indy is in a daze and is going to hurt his friends. Luckily, quick-thinking Short Round comes to his rescue!

Short Round
Short Round is a young orphan from Shanghai. He cures Indy by burning him—the shock snaps Indy out of his zombie sleep.

As Indy runs from his enemies, he is almost stabbed by a rhino horn before falling into a box of snakes.

Slippery foes

All his life, Indy has had trouble with one thing: snakes. As a boy, he fought a battle on a moving circus train. During the struggle, Indy fell into a box full of snakes. Since then, he has been quite afraid of them!

Even as a grown-up, Dr. Jones is still very scared of snakes.

While looking for the Crystal Skull, Indy begins to sink into a sand pit. His son, Mutt, throws him a line. Unfortunately, it's a snake! Indy thinks he might prefer to stay in the sand pit...

Horse helpers

Indy might have a problem with snakes, but he is not afraid of other animals. In fact, he is particularly fond of horses and has learned to ride them very well and at high speeds. This skill has helped him escape from danger many times in his life.

Young Indy rode a horse to escape grave robbers.

When he is older, Indy jumps from his white horse onto a truck

Indy is not afraid to do battle with a truckload of Nazis.

to recapture the Ark of the Covenant.

Even as a young man, Indy had to escape from danger many times.

Which way out?

Escape can mean trying to find an exit even if it looks like there is no way out.

Inside Club Obi Wan, Indy and Willie Scott are in a fight with gangsters. Indy has been poisoned and he is trying to find a small vial of the antidote.

Willie Scott
Nightclub singer Willie is not looking for adventure when she meets Indiana. She just wants to earn enough money to travel back to America in style.

Dancing girls are on the stage. Bad guys are shooting at Indy and Willie, but Willie has found the antidote. Indy grabs Willie and runs. They crash through a window and jump into a waiting car. What an escape!

Indy has another problem. He has found the Ark of the Covenant, but he and Marion are stuck in a tomb. There is no exit—they have been sealed in.

Indy balances on the statue's head

Wait a second! Indy sees a snake slithering out of a wall, so there must be a way out through that wall. He climbs up a giant statue of a jackal and makes the statue crash through the wall. Indy and Marion have escaped again!

Ark of the Covenant
The Hebrew prophet Moses is believed to have placed the tablets containing the Ten Commandments in the Ark.

Head for heights

It is a good thing Indy is not afraid of heights. Indy, Willie, and Short Round are chased by angry Thuggees and end up on a steep cliff with nowhere to go. They can escape only by climbing up the cliff wall, although falling would mean certain death!

Thuggees are still chasing Indy.
They have trapped him on a flimsy
rope-bridge high above a river filled
with man-eating crocodiles.

How does Indy escape?
He ties himself to the rope-bridge,
slashes the thick cords with his sword,
and swings to safety!

Narrow escape

Sometimes, every second counts when it comes to making an escape.

Indy is trying to rescue Marion from a Nazi plane, but a tough mechanic is

Once again Indy has to use his fists!

determined to stop him. Gasoline is leaking from the plane and spreading toward a fire.

Indy defeats the giant mechanic, and then blasts the cockpit's lock with his pistol to rescue Marion. But the flames have already ignited the gasoline.

There are only seconds to spare until Indy and Marion meet a fiery end. The plane explodes as they both have to run for their lives!

Lessons from the past

Indiana has been facing dangerous foes for much of his life. He has learned to stay cool in a crisis, even though he wasn't always that way.

Young Indy was a spy during World War I. He was attacked by a flying ace known as the Red Baron and taken prisoner at gunpoint. He was very afraid.

Years later, the villain
Walter Donovan and his
men pull their guns on
Indy. However, Indy is

*Young Indy is
taken prisoner*

no longer afraid and Donovan has to
find another way to make Indy do what
he wants. So, Donovan wounds Indy's
father—now to save his father Indy
must find the Holy Grail for his enemy.

Disguise

Indy's face is well known to his enemies, so he has to create disguises to escape.

Indy is on the trail of the Ark of the Covenant, which has been hidden in a submarine. Indy swims from his ship to the submarine and travels on board to a mysterious island.

Indy sneaks off the submarine. He ambushes a Nazi and steals his uniform, but it is too small. Luckily

Marion Ravenwood is also a prisoner on the submarine.

another officer arrives and his uniform fits Indy perfectly. Now he can escape!

Master of disguise
When searching for the Ark, Indy also has to sneak into a Nazi camp, so he disguises himself as an Arab worker to avoid detection.

Look away!

Sometimes escaping has nothing to do with running away or firing powerful weapons. It comes down to good sense and quick thinking.

When Belloq opens the Ark of the Covenant, vengeful spirits appear. They make the lights explode and then they destroy Belloq and his Nazi thugs.

The spirits are angry and threaten to consume even Indy and Marion. Indy quickly tells Marion to close her eyes and they are spared. Indiana Jones has done it once again. He always manages to make a great escape!

Marion's father, Abner, had warned Indy that the Ark was dangerous.

Glossary

Ancient
Something that is very old.

Antidote
The cure for a poisonous bite.

Archaeologist
Someone who studies ancient life and objects.

Assassin
A person who is employed to kill someone.

Bazooka
A shoulder-held weapon, which fires rockets.

Cloud Forests
A tropical forest that is mostly covered by cloud.

Descendants
The offspring of a particular person or family.

Diabolical
Very bad or evil.

Exotic
Somewhere far away with a different culture.

Feisty
Strong and opinionated.

Henchmen
Trusted followers.

Idol
A statue that is worshipped as a god.

Ignited
Set on fire.

Invaluable
Extremely useful or priceless.

Jackal
An animal that is similar to a dog.

Miraculous
An event which has no rational explanation.

Perilous
Extremely scary and dangerous.

Plummeted
Fell suddenly and steeply.

Sacred
Something holy.

Scimitar
A type of curved sword.

Thuggees
Members of the Thuggee cult.

Tomb
A cave used for burial.

Trench
A ditch where soldiers hide from enemy attack.

Vampire
A being that drinks human blood.

Vial
A small, sealed container.

Zombie
A dead body brought back to life.

Index